Good Night
Mia and the Moon
It's Almost Bedtime

A Magnificent Me! estorytime.com Series

by

Melissa Ryan

ISBN-13: 978-1541157507

ISBN-10: 1541157508

Dedication

"To all the Mia's in the land...sweet dreams...sleep tight...
Love you...good night."

Goodnight Mia
And the Moon.
It's Almost Bedtime.

It's time to get into your cozy warm bed.

Of course, you'll need your dolly by your side. Before you go to sleep Mia, let's say good night to everything in the house.

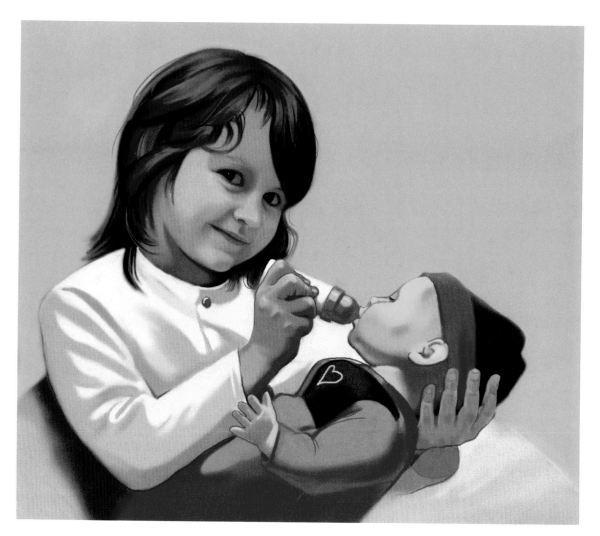

First, you need to say good night to your rocking chair Mia. Good night, rocking chair. You need to get some rest after rocking my baby dolly and me today.

Can you believe it? I've been between your arms since I was a tiny baby. Rock-a-rock-a-bye rocking chair. Sweet dreams.

Goodnight Mia
And the Moon.
It's Almost Bedtime.

It's time to get into your cozy warm bed.

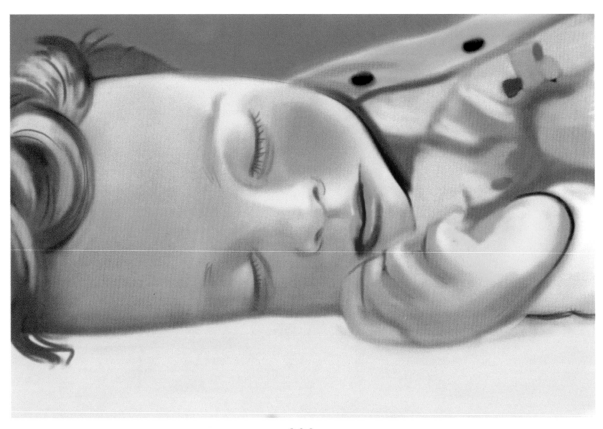

Of course, you'll need your dolly by your side. Before you go to sleep Mia, let's say good night to everything in the house.

Let's go to the kitchen, Mia!

Now, let's say good night to the kitchen table, Mia. Good night, kitchen table. I love to be around you every day—eating yummy food. I'm a BIG girl now 'cuz I use a BIG girl fork!

Do you remember when I ate our secret special spaghetti?

I had it all over my face. I love noodles!

Silly Mia Spaghetti Face!

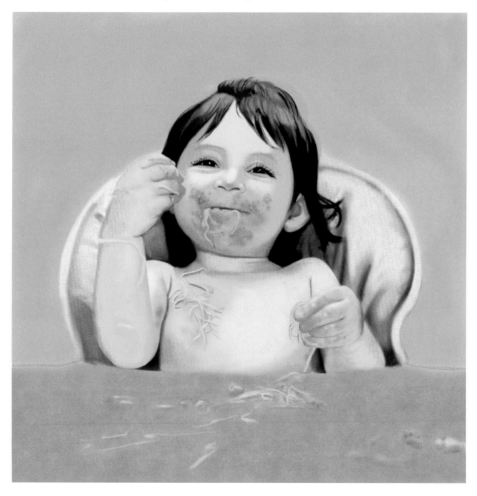

I really love when we bake Mia sweet sugar cookies! We both get flour all over us. We talk around you for hours and no one ever wants to leave your side. Sweet dreams, kitchen table.

Goodnight Mia
And the Moon.
It's Almost Bedtime.

It's time to get into your cozy warm bed.

Of course, you'll need your dolly by your side. Before you go to sleep Mia, let's say good night to everything in the house.

Let's go find your bathtub, Mia!

Now it's time to say good night to your bathtub. Good night, bathtub.
Do you remember when I was covered in mud after I played outside?
You were just as muddy as me! Our bath time is so much fun!

Or what about when I was a painter and "painted" myself?
You were painted too! I love paint brushes and paint!
Mommy told me we were both washable.

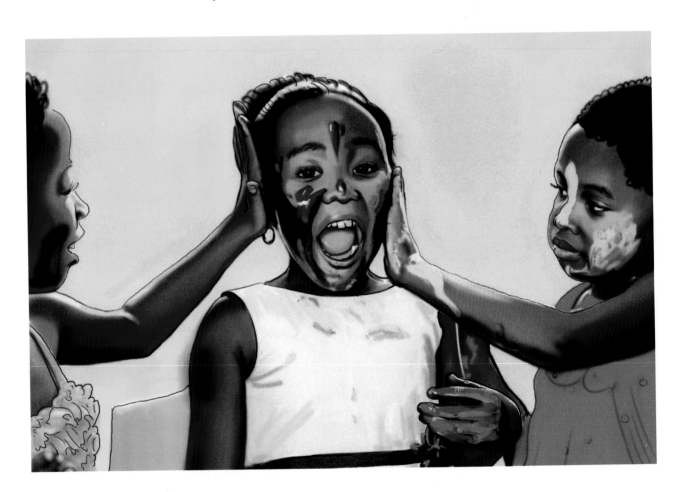

Do you remember my very first bath?
I looked so tiny and the tub seemed so big! Little Baby Mia!

I was a slippy-slidey-wiggle-giggle Mia.
Sweet dreams, bathtub

Goodnight Mia
And the Moon.
It's Almost Bedtime.

It's time to get into your cozy warm bed.

Of course, you'll need your dolly by your side. Before you go to sleep Mia, let's say good night to everything in the house.

Where's your toothbrush, Mia?

Now it's time to say good night to your scrubby, dubby toothbrush. Good night, toothbrush. Thanks for helping me clean my teeth every night before I go to sleep.

You have such a pretty smile, Mia!

I like holding you in my hand and putting my pink toothpaste on.
Add some water, and you are magic!
Bubble Pop! Mia's mouth tickles!

You always make my teeth so white and shiny.

Up and down. Back and forth. Round and round. Top teeth. Bottom teeth. Swish!

Now it's time to lie you down to go to sleep. You've had a busy day today. Sweet dreams, toothbrush.

Goodnight Mia
And the Moon.
It's Almost Bedtime.

It's time to get into your cozy warm bed.

• • •

Of course, you'll need your dolly by your side. Before you go to sleep Mia, let's say good night to everything in the house.

Where is your bed Mia? Let's go find it together!

Now it's finally time to say good night to your warm, cozy bed. Good night, bed. Thanks for giving me somewhere soft to lay my head every night.

I have the sweetest Mia dreams whenever I'm with you.

You're with me when I'm read my favorite bedtime story over and over again. You're with me when Mommy lays beside me after I wake up and need a hug.

• • •

You always make me feel warm and fuzzy. You're with me on cold winter days when you're extra warm, and I am snuggled in. You stick right by my side when my tummy hurts and I don't feel good. Now it's your turn for sweet dreams, warm and cozy bed.

Goodnight Mia
And the Moon.
It's Almost Bedtime.

It's time to get into your cozy warm bed.

Of course, you'll need your dolly by your side. Before you go to sleep Mia, let's say good night to everything in the house.

Where am I, Mia? Let's curl up and cuddle together.

Now it's time for me to say good night to you. Good night, sweet Mia. Everything is ready for bed, including you.

Close your eyes dear Mia, and think of all the things that make you happy. Think of all the great memories you made today, and the fun you will have tomorrow, and every day after that.

Think of where you will go in your dreams. Mia, will you dream of dancing on a fluffy white cotton candy cloud and draw a rainbow with your finger?

Or will you hold a butterfly in your hand, resting in a field of yellow flowers? Mia, blow gently on her wings and watch her fly through the sky like you in your dreams.

Flittering and flying, such a sweet butterfly.

Tomorrow is a new adventure. Good night Mia and the Moon. It is now bedtime. Sweetest of dreams. I love you.

Did you like this book?

I really get excited and encouraged by positive reviews of this

book and would appreciate your taking 30 seconds out of your day to give it a review at Amazon.   Be sure to let your friends know about the estorytime book series. Thank you!

Storytime continues . . .

Follow the adventures of Mia at: http://estorytime.com

Stay in touch with the author via: melissa@estorytime.com

Don't Forget! Personalization Available!

If you would like to order this estorybook personalized in another child's name, please go to our website and send an email through our Contact or Personalization page. Simply pick the estorybook title you'd like, give us your child's first name, and that's it! We will email you to let you know when the book is available for ordering on Amazon!

About The Author

Melissa Ryan...

is a Mom of five kids, and we all enjoy a love of reading. From my family to yours, and to sweet Mia... enjoy.

Made in the USA
Middletown, DE
03 August 2018